CROSSWINDS PRESS, INC.
P.O. Box 683
Mystic, Connecticut 06355
crosswindspress.com

Printed in the United States of America

ISBN 978-0-9825559-2-7

10 9 8 7 6 5 4 3 2 1

Book design by Trish Sinsigalli LaPointe, LaPointe Design.
Old Mystic, Connecticut
tslapointedesign.com

Printed by The Racine Company
Brooklyn, Connecticut
racinecompany.com

Printed on environmentally friendly,
silk coated, acid-free, archival paper.

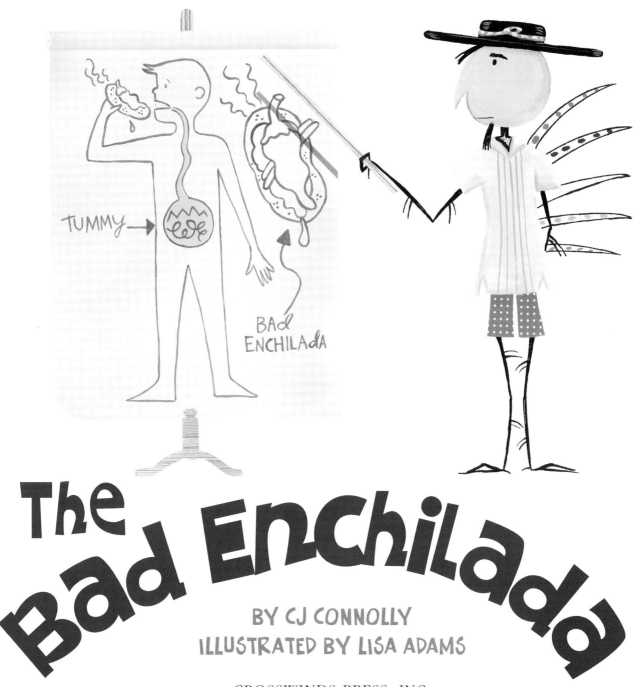

The Bad Enchilada

BY CJ CONNOLLY
ILLUSTRATED BY LISA ADAMS

CROSSWINDS PRESS, INC.

To George, whose encouragement, commitment
and love make anything possible....

Prologue

The Bad Enchilada is the third book in the series that began with *Wil, Fitz and a Flea Named "T."* Mr. T is a wise old flea, a modern day Jiminy Cricket, that has decided to help Wil learn a few of life's lessons while having fun along the way.

As might be expected, Mr. T has a lot of relatives who tend to visit more often than Fitz, Wil's dog, would probably like. They all bear names made up of letters (anywhere from one to twenty-three) that provide insight into their personality and the adventure to come. In this book, Mr. T's Mexican nephew "CC" helps Wil see that if you don't let go of anger, it causes "indigestion," just like a bad enchilada! Enjoy!

"Rodger, Dodger," shouted Wil
"Bring your truck over the hill!"
And Donny did just that and more…
He came over the hill with a mighty roar!

Then Wil and Donny moved dirt and rocks,
Building up a mighty stock.
It was Saturday...play day...what a joy!
Fun for everyone, girl or boy!

While the commotion built and laughter rose,
Mr. T continued sleeping on Fitz's nose.
He'd seen the game before, my friend...
Demolition derby would be the end.

The action continued and the noise it rose higher
As Mr. T got a visitor, no it wasn't a spider!
It was his Mexican nephew, "CC" was his name…
He was making his way thru Fitz's shaggy mane.

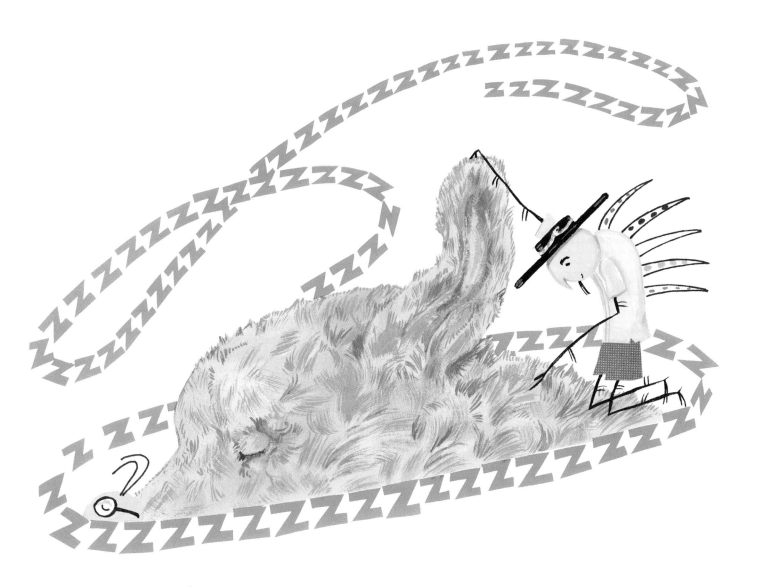

"Tio T, Tio T, are you anywhere about?"
CC was concerned, so he started to shout.
"Tio T, Tio T are you under Fitz's ear?
Is that why my greetings you cannot hear?"

Mr. T snuffled, and grumbled, then harummphed in reply.
"I'm up on Fitz's nose to avoid all the flies!
Do you need me to fetch you or can you find your way?
Hope it's the latter, as I'm catching some rays!"

"I can find you, Tio T," said CC with a smile.
"I'm here for a visit, I'll stay a short while...
It's sleepy in Tijuana, so I decided to travel.
To learn from watching the secrets you unravel."

"Are you sure you're my nephew or is it a joke?
For 'si-si' is a very strange name for a bloke.
Saying yes all the time would be bothersome to me,"
Was the welcome that greeted poor little CC.

"Uncle T, or Tio T, as I normally would say,
I'm not saying yes, no….'C' 'C' is my name.
One simple letter that appears together twice,
Has proven to be the bane of my life!"

"Tut, tut my lad, don't be so down-hearted.
Your name is a positive for once it is started,
It leads to the future, for 'yes' is the way,
To begin something new, to have fun, to play!"

"You are right, Tio T, as you usually are,
Perhaps I'll start thinking I'm just like a star!
'Cause it's true that I'm always ready for action,
I seldom say 'no,' 'yes-yes' is my reaction!"

As T and CC continued to chat,
Wil and Donny were having a terrible spat.
Seems both of them wanted to be the brave knight,
But the ogre? Oh no! What an ugly sight!

"Wil, you're a better ogre than me…"
Said Donny in earnest as he kicked at a tree.
"You roar so much louder, you're stronger, you're tough,
I'm actually too little—not near big enough!"

"Are you saying I'm bigger or meaner or what?"
Wil demanded an answer, he was in a big huff!
"Or are you simply tricking me to act like a beast,
If that is the case, our playing will cease!"

The tension built and the friends began glaring,
In all of the mayhem they forgot about caring.
They stomped off instead, both angry, so mad!
Seems play time was over…good times had turned bad.

T watched from Fitz's nose and pondered again,
Why it was so hard for cousins to stay friends?
"CC, do you see what has happened today?
What should we do to get them to play?"

CC scratched his head, then looked low and high,
Hoping that an answer into his brain would fly.
He tried to look thoughtful, like a smart little flea,
Then he came up with an answer for dear Tio T!

"Tio T, I've been watching with concern your friend Wil,
He's not very happy…No he's quite angry still.
At Donny for a comment, a slight Wil's perceived,
It's left him upset, in fact he is peeved!"

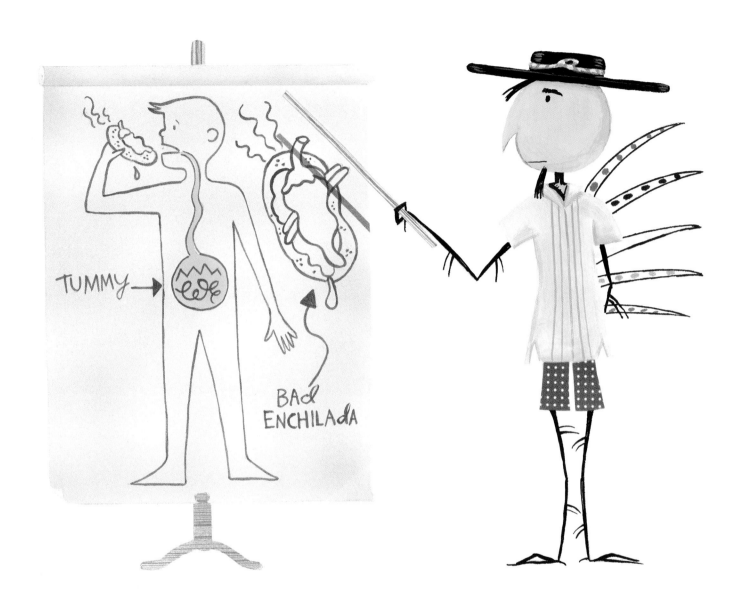

"His anger, it seems, is just like Mexican food,
Enchiladas in fact, a quite yummy stew!
But when they are bad they can cause much distress,
A bad enchilada makes your tummy a mess!"

"You eat a bad enchilada once but taste it more,
It keeps coming back, like a canker sore!
'BURP, BELCH, BURP' is all you can say,
As the bad enchilada ruins your day!"

"I believe, Tio T, that Wil's regurgitating,
The words and feelings that arose from Donny stating
That Wil was a better ogre than he,
It's stuck in Wil's craw, he can't get it free!"

"Not bad, my lad, I can see what you're saying,
Now let's see if Wil can be talked into playing."
T walked to the end of Fitz's nose and did yell,
"Say Wil, come on over, I've a story to tell!"

Wil heard Mr. T, but pretended he didn't…
So T shouted more loudly, not for seconds but minutes.
Wil finally gave in, wandered over and stared,
At T and his nephew, they made quite a pair.

"What do you want, T? Who's that by your side?
Fitz doesn't need more fleas…where will they all hide?
Anyway, I'm quite busy," said Wil as he turned,
It seemed Mr. T was about to be spurned!

"Wil, meet my nephew, his name is 'CC'.
It seems he has a question that's stumped poor ol' T.
He wants to know if you've ever had a bad enchilada,
One that was greasy, and gooey, dripping with salsa?"

"What a nutty question, T, has he lost all his marbles?"
"Yes I've had a bad enchilada," said Wil slightly garbled.
"It was gooey and slimy and made me quite queasy,
I burped it for hours, it was awfully greasy!"

"As you burped up that bad enchilada," asked T,
"Did it make you feel woozy, did it make you quite green?
You wanted it to go away, but it stayed nonetheless…
Making your tummy and head quite a mess."

"Now ponder for me Wil and think upon
The fight you're having with your cousin Don.
Does the anger keep coming back, it simply won't go away?
'Cause it seems that's the case…and it's ruining your day!"

"So I want you to count to ten and then three,
And with each new number your anger let free.
Before you know it you'll be happy once more,
No more enchilada! No more salsa to pour!"

So Wil took a deep breath, winking fondly at T,
He counted and counted 'til he finally felt free…
Then he ran over to Donny who sat sadly, alone,
And gave him a big hug—his anger atoned.

Bad feelings and bitterness can go on for hours,
And when they are present you can't smell the flowers.
So let go of your anger, your distrust, your fear…
Only then towards happiness can your heart be steered.